Lucy and The Beauty Queen
🎁 A GIFTED GIRLS® SERIES   Book 2

Lucy
AND THE
Beauty Queen

By
Victoria London

Cover Illustration
By
Angela Liang

Published by Sparklesoup Studios, Inc.

Copyright © 2002 by Kailin Gow for Victoria London

Published by Sparklesoup Studios

09-1610
Sparkle Soup
(Amazon)
6/09
6.95

For information, please contact:
Sparklesoup Studios
P.O. Box 2285
Frisco, TX 75034

First Edition.

Printed in the United States of America.

Library of Congress Cataloging-in-Publication Data

London, Victoria, 1970-

Lucy And The Beauty Queen: Book 2 / by Victoria London; illustrations, Angela Liang - 1st ed.

p. cm. - (Gifted Girls Series)

Summary: After finding out that she has an extraodinary magical gift from God, modern-day Lucy uses it to help a friend out in school, only to find out through her journeys back in time to ancient Egypt and her adventures with a teenage Cleopatra, that some things are better left alone.

ISBN: 0-9714776-1-2

1. World-History-Cleopatra - Juvenile fiction.

[1. World-History-Cleopatra-Fiction. 2. Fantasy-Juvenile fiction. 3. Friendship-fiction.]

This book belongs to:

_____

This book is dedicated to Lucy, who lives life with passion and zest; to Paul, whose generosity and integrity is beyond the grasp of common man; to James, a most generous man; to Angela, a new mother; to Linda and Quinn, whose commitment to family transcends years; to Tam, who is my second Mom; to Bonnie, whose whole-hearted enthusiasm of the book encouraged me to seek wider distribution; to my "test" group who loved the Gifted Girls® idea; and to my wonderful husband Finlay, who makes this series possible.

Table of Contents

God has given everyone gifts and talents. It is the one and only Holy Spirit who distributes these gifts. He alone decides which gift each person should have.

1 Corinthians 12:11

Chapter One

The Quest: Egypt 1954

The room grew dark, and I found myself no longer in the comforts of my sunshine yellow bedroom in modern-day Southern California, but outside in the middle of a desert. A red sun about to set, stared straight at me. The path went up and down, up and down.

"Go," a dark man dressed in a long brown cotton robe said as he stood next to me. He slapped the animal I was riding on to move faster. I glanced down. A large tan furry head with large bulbous eyes glanced back at me. I was riding on top of a camel!

I looked around me. There were other people riding on top of camels beside me. An older man with wild white hair and a white beard, a young woman with long wavy auburn hair, a thin-faced man with a patch over his right eye, a brawny young man with blond hair, and a finely-dressed young man with wavy brown hair. Except for the brown-haired young man, everyone was dressed from head to toe as I was: khakis and jackets with hiking boots and safari hats. Dark men dressed in long brown robes walked besides each camel, urging them forward. Some camels carried boxes of supplies.

"Excuse me," I whispered to the young woman with wavy auburn hair, "do you know where we're going?"

The young woman laughed, "If my calculations are correct, we should be heading straight to the Hidden

Tomb of Egypt's most famous Queen... Cleopatra."

"Cleopatra?" I asked. "As in the Queen of the Nile?"

"Yes," the beautiful young woman said with an unmistakable British accent. "I see you've actually cracked open your history book for once, my young Cousin Lucy," she joked.

"Muriel!" the old man with the wild white hair shouted. "The men are getting hungry, and it's getting late. We have to make a stop soon."

"Alright, Father," Muriel shouted back. "I could go on and on, can't you?" She took a deep breath. "I love this Egyptian open air. Quite a change from the stuffy, drafty London air we have back home."

The well-dress young man wearing a sports coat and riding pants rode his camel up to Muriel and I. "Muriel," he said politely. "I wouldn't want anything to happen to you all alone out here with all of these men and nasty animals. I'd like to suggest that you pitch your tent next to mine."

Muriel's back straightened. "I'm perfectly capable of taking care of myself, thank you, Roger," she said firmly, "And I'm not 'here all alone' like you said." She smiled. "Have you forgotten, I have my cousin Lucy with me!"

I looked over at Roger and smiled my widest, smuggest smile. Roger's lips curled, and he left without a word of good-bye. Muriel and I looked at each other and burst into laughter.

The group of travelers and camel handlers soon came to a stop at the foot of a cliff with some palm trees.

As we got off our camels, and the men began setting up camp, I wandered near the palm trees, searching for water. A few feet away from the trees, I found a swimming hole with fruit trees and birds. As I reached up to grab one of the ripe black figs from one of the trees, I heard Muriel's voice shout, "Watch out, Lucy!"

I looked up to see Muriel's anxious face looking at the fig I was holding, only this time I realized it was not a fig but a large, fuzzy poisonous tarantula spider as big as my hand!

"Don't move," Muriel said. She reached into her leather satchel and pulled out a thick leather glove and walked towards me, placing the glove on her right hand. When she reached me, she quickly grabbed the spider from me, and placed it on a rock.

Muriel smiled. "Now you can move, but away from the spider, mind you."

"Thanks," I said, breathing in a sigh of relief. I looked around. The trees and the garden were no longer there. "Where did the garden go?" I asked. "With the pool of water, fruit trees, birds…"

"You must have seen a mirage," Muriel laughed. "Not too uncommon to see one in the middle of a desert, I'm sure." She wrinkled her small nose and joked, "That would explain why you bravely, if not insanely, reached for that large tarantula."

"I thought it was a fig!" I protested, my cheeks becoming flushed with embarrassment.

"Luckily it wasn't poisonous," Muriel said. "Tarantulas only look poisonous, but, they are not. They can be very dangerous, though."

"How dangerous?" I asked, my eyes widening. I wanted to know how foolish I had been, often torturing myself with unnecessary thoughts of gloom and pain.

"Well," Muriel said slowly, her brilliant blue eyes shining with mischief. "They have…very sharp teeth!" With that she made a pair of fangs with her two index fingers and leapt towards me.

I let out a scream that would have awoken the dead. Then Muriel had her arms around me, hugging me and laughing. I started laughing with her, embarrassed to be scared so easily, especially since I was 12-years-old, much too old to be scared silly.

"Hey!" a shout came from nearby. It was the blond-haired young man in the group. "Is everything alright?" he asked as he started walking towards us. He didn't have a British lilt like Muriel, Muriel's father, or Roger.

Muriel stopped laughing. "Oh, not to worry, Peter. Everything is fine."

"I thought I heard a scream," Peter said, his handsome face still looking worried.

"Oh, we were just having some bit of fun," Muriel said lightly. "Something you Americans ought to do more often!" Muriel teased.

Now it was Peter's turn to look embarrassed. "I... well, since you ladies are fine, I will be heading back to camp," he muttered, his eyes looking down.

"Whoa!" another shout came from the direction of the camp. Then Muriel's father and the thin man with an eye-patch moved closer to us from over the hill. "What in tarnations is all this commotion?" Muriel's father asked.

"Just having some light fun," Muriel said, starting to look embarrassed herself now.

"To ease all the tension," I interrupted.

Muriel looked at me with gratefulness in her eyes. "After all, we *have* been riding all day in the sun."

The thin man looked disapprovingly at Muriel, Peter, and I. "I did not fund this expedition so that a bunch of little girls can have some fun!" He looked at Muriel's father. "Dr. Winston, I expect to find this tomb by tomorrow at the latest! And as I said before, this is no place for women!"

"But Mr. Randolph, Muriel knows more about Cleopatra than anyone I know. She excels above all students, both men and women, in her classes at the university." Muriel's father replied.

Mr. Randolph turned angrily towards him and pointed his crooked finger in his face. "I said tomorrow at the latest or this expedition is over! I do not care who leads this expedition, Miss Winston or even one of the camel handlers, preferably not Miss Winston, but you have until tomorrow!" Then he threw another look of disgust at Muriel before he left.

I looked at Muriel. She had her head down and remained quiet. I looked at Dr. Winston and Peter, who looked helplessly at Muriel, not knowing what to do. Finally Dr. Winston walked up to Muriel and placed a hand on her shoulder. "It is alright, my girl," he said. "Your first expedition - and only at 18 years old! I did not get to go on my first expedition until I was near 40. You were just 5 years old then...."

I walked over to Peter, who looked uncomfortable standing there amidst all the emotions.

Then I heard some sniffling. Muriel. Only it was not sniffling, but a low chuckling.

"Drat that man!" Muriel said. "Not believing a woman can lead this expedition! You would have thought he lived in the 19th century and not in the year 1954!"

I stopped all movement and froze in my spot. 1954? When I had put on my safari outfit earlier today, I was in my room in Huntington Beach, California, and it was September 2001. I reached up and touched my golden necklace. Its heart shape and golden bowtie sparkled in the dimming lights of dusk. It was still there, thank goodness! A gift delivered by the merry Mrs. Potts, who helped me discover that I was a Gifted Girl with a gift for sewing. I shook my head in disbelief. When I had put on my safari outfit and magical necklace today, I was hoping it would transport me to the year 1994 to the jungles where my archaeologist father disappeared. Apparently, I still have much to learn about using my gifts.

"Listen," Muriel said excitedly to Dr. Winston, Peter, and I. "I was just studying the pattern of the sun on the sand before it sets, and I think we're not too far from the tomb." Then the color of her ocean blue eyes deepened with excitement. "And I bet we will find it tomorrow morning if we set out at the first sight of dawn." Her chuckling became louder.

"I sure hope so," Dr. Winston said, running a hand through his wild white mane.

"I could swear we are extremely close." Muriel pulled out a brown crumpled cloth. Everyone drew close around her. "According to this ancient map, the Queen's tomb is near a hill facing east of the river. The Nile River." Muriel read the colorful inscriptions on the map. "In the Valley of the Kings."

Peter let out a whistle. "What a woman!" Everyone stared blankly at him. It was the second time Peter blushed. "I mean… That she was a queen, but she was to be buried as a king."

Muriel smiled. "But she fell in love with Mark Antony, a Roman ruler, and was buried with him when she died. No one knows where they are buried, but I venture to guess that her tomb is outside of the ancient city of Alexandria and was thus spared the city's fate - crumbling into the sea."

"You mean we may actually uncover Cleopatra herself?" I asked, "With Mark Antony?"

"Actually, I don't think they were buried in her tomb," Muriel said, "but it would be worth uncovering anything that belongs to her to learn more about her and the time period she lived in." Muriel stopped. The remaining sunlight had vanished, and the darkness of the desert was slowly enveloping us.

Peter muttered, "Let's head back to camp. I thought

I saw a shadow."

I looked around me and noticed that there were several shadows now. I guess Peter, Muriel, and Dr. Winston had noticed too because we quickened our pace up towards the hill heading for the campground.

When we reached the campground at the base of a small cliff, Roger and Mr. Randolph was frantically running around. "Those thieves!" shouted Roger, "They took all our supplies!"

Mr. Randolph piped in, "And our camels! Camel handlers, indeed!"

"Now, now," Dr. Winston reassured. "We can get fresh supplies tomorrow...after we find Cleopatra's tomb."

Mr. Randolph and Roger grew silent.

Muriel said, "That's right! We're within yards maybe. If we get some rest tonight, and rise at the first crack of dawn, we can find it within hours."

I piped in, "Boy, sleep and food sounds good, doesn't it? Speaking about food, what do we have to eat?" I walked up to a steaming pot and looked inside. Peter followed me.

"Looks like the thieves at least made us some dinner." Then he lifted the ladle and poured some porridge into his mouth. "Umm, tasty," he said. "Since we don't have any bowls or utensils, I'm just going to eat it this way. Want to try?"

"Sure," I said. With that, I opened my mouth, and Peter poured a ladleful of gruel in. It was spicy, but filling. I still missed my grandmother's Chinese food, though.

"Uggh," Roger said. "I'll pass." He looked at Muriel. "Perhaps you would like to come with me to search for something more palatable?"

"This is just fine," Muriel said, opening her mouth wide open and accepting a ladleful of gruel from Peter. "This is good," she said.

Roger said, "Fine. I'll just go join my uncle. At least he is civilized." Then he left in a huff.

Peter shook his head. "I don't know about you British folks, but what is it with this 'civilized' and 'uncivilized' business? Seems to me when you're in Rome, you do as the Romans do. Back home in Kentucky, everyone follows the land. Whether you raise horses or grow crops, you learn to respect the land." Peter took the pot away from the pit and struck some flint. Soon a roaring fire started.

"Sounds beautiful," Muriel said. "Don't you worry about Roger, though," she said softly, "he's just like his uncle Mr. Randolph, thinking that money can buy everything, even love...."

Staring into the fire, I felt warm and sleepy. As I fell asleep, I missed the glances Muriel and Peter exchanged.

* * *

I awoke to the sound of shuffling. "Shhh," a feminine voice said. It was Muriel. "It is almost the crack of daylight. Let's not wake the others," she said. "Come with me."

I got up and realized I was wearing a coat. Muriel saw my surprised look. "You were shivering so I let you have mine." Then she proceeded to whisper, as we got further away from the camp towards the hill where I had previously envisioned a mirage. "It was underneath our noses all this time," she explained. "Cleopatra's tomb. Thousands of years ago, this desert looked different. There were palm trees around here, an oasis, and birds. Maybe your mirage wasn't a mirage at all, but a vision." She touched my nose. "Thousands of years have weathered this hill, but I think this is the hill on the map, and if I'm right..." said Muriel as she walked a few steps further.

At that moment, a shadow appeared before us. A man in a dark robe darted before us - one of the camel handlers. Something shiny glinted in his hand. "Madam, I believe you have something I want," he said.

Muriel stared icily back at him. "You took everything we have, our camels, our equipment!"

The man smiled in the dark. "But you have a map to the Valley of the Kings." The man's sinister grin widened, "There should be many riches to be had. Several tombs to explore." He stopped smiling and in a threatening growl, commanded. "Give me the map!"

"I left it at the camp," Muriel said.

"Impossible! With something so precious, you would have it on you. Give me the map!" the menacing figure threatened.

At that moment, Muriel did something I had only seen in movies. She jumped up and kicked the knife out of the man's hand. "Lucy, run for help!"

I started running, but the man leapt at me like a football player and tackled my legs. I fell to the ground. As I fell to the floor, my hand flew up and brushed against the golden heart necklace. Before I blanked out, I prayed for safety. As promised, my prayer was answered.

Chapter Two

The Girl Who Did Not Exist

My adventure in 1954 ended as soon as it had began. I was back in my room in California, lying on the soft beige carpet in front of my closet in the same position as when I fell and blanked out in Egypt. I quickly got up and checked myself in the full-length pine mirror. I looked the same - long dark hair, dark almond-shaped eyes, oval face… but my face was flushed, and I had beads of sweat covering my forehead. It seemed like a dream, yet it felt so *real*. Maybe it was a dream.

I looked down. I had on the tailored safari khaki coat Muriel had given me. I reached into my left inside pocket and felt a soft thin material. I pulled it out. It was Muriel's ancient map. My heart raced. It wasn't a dream, and everything Mrs. Potts said about me being one of the Gifted Girls was true. I had to return the map to Muriel or she would never be able to find Cleopatra's tomb.

A knock startled me out of making a decision to go back. "Well, is anyone home?" a little boy's voice resonated from the hallway outside my bedroom.

I sighed. Nothing like my brother Peter bringing me back to present day. I opened the door, and a little 7-year-old boy in Batman pajamas ran in. "Your boyfriend and his sister are waiting outside in a car. They're going to take you to school today."

"My boyfriend?" I asked. What boyfriend?

"Yeah," Peter said. "That tall blond boy who was here with his soured-face sister a couple of days ago."

"Oh, Josh and Jenny," I said. "He is *not* my

boyfriend," I told Peter squarely, although I secretly thought Josh was the world's cutest boy. "We are just friends."

"Whatever you say," Peter said. "He's out there in a nice black Jaguar!"

I looked out my window to the front of my house. Sure enough a black luxury car was pulled up in front. "I gotta get ready!" I said, quickly brushing my hair, brushing my teeth, and washing my face. "Gotta change." I said to Peter. "Out!"

I quickly changed into a light blue skirt suit and put a gingham light blue and white headband in my hair. There - I looked polished enough. I grabbed my backpack on the floor, raced down the stairs to the kitchen, grabbed a banana and my lunch bag.

Mom was in the kitchen, drinking coffee with Grandma. "Slow down, Lucy," Mom said.

"I'm late already. Gotta go!" I said, kissing Mom and Grandma good-bye. I rushed out the door, and headed for the black Jaguar. Josh was already standing outside with the door open.

"Hi Lucy," he said with a smile. "We thought it would be nice to give you a lift to school since we're not too far from here."

His sister Jenny said, "It's along the way."

Josh took my backpack, and I scooted in next to Jenny. "Nice car," I said smiling.

"Thanks!" a deep feminine voice said. "I'm glad you like this car."

"Oh," Josh said, "Lucy, this is Mom. Mom, you know Lucy..."

"Nice to meet you, Mrs. Cromwell," I said to the pretty blond woman driving the beautiful car.

"Same here," she said. "Josh and Jenny has been telling me all about you! Hope you enjoy California. It's not easy moving to a new place and having to make new friends."

"I know," I said. "But now, I have two more friends than before," I said smiling at Josh and Jenny. They smiled back. At that moment, they almost looked like twins, although Josh was two years older than Jenny and I.

"You two didn't tell me how sweet Lucy is, too," Mrs. Cromwell said.

"Didn't need to," Josh said, always the gentleman. "Her actions speak for themselves."

I blushed. Why do I feel so self-conscious when Josh says anything about me? Shoot, why do I feel so self-conscious when Josh says anything *to* me? I wonder if Josie or Rachel, my closest girlfriends back in New York, also feel this way about boys or am I the only one? The black Jaguar came to a stop just in front of our school, Beachside Middle School. Josh got out of the car and opened the door for my side. "Thanks for the ride!" I told Mrs. Cromwell. "It was very nice meeting you."

Mrs. Cromwell said quickly, "Guys, I'll be waiting back here at 3. Don't be late! Jenny has her piano lessons to go to."

"Okay," Josh replied. "Bye, Mom!"

"Bye, Mom!" Jenny said, joining Josh and I outside. Josh soon left us as he went to join his 8th grade friends. Jenny and I walked together down the hall towards our history class. Before we entered, a tall girl with brown pigtails and thick glasses came crashing into us.

"I'm sorry," she mumbled looking down. "One of the boys tripped me," she said dejectedly.

"How clumsy," Jenny said, adjusting her pink sweater and khaki pants.

"That's alright," I said, giving Jenny my *what-are-you-doing?!!* look. Even though Jenny and I are now friends, thanks to Josh, not too long ago she was not very nice to me as well. "Let me help you up," I said, pulling myself up and lending her a helping hand.

The tall girl accepted. "Thanks," she said.

"No problem," I said, smiling. "My name's Lucy Lee."

"I'm Cornelia Ham, but everyone, I mean everyone in my family, calls me Nellie." She stopped suddenly. "I better go," she said sadly. Then she stumbled off, her shoulders hunched forward, feet shuffling.

"Isn't she the most uncool thing there is?" Jenny asked, looking at Nellie's dejected awkward figure disappear into oblivion. "No wonder nobody knows who she is."

"Hey guys!" Renee shouted from down the hall. "Wait up!" She ran up to us. Even though I shared more classes with Jenny, Renee and I became instant friends the first day of school for me. She was friendly and down-to-earth like my New York friends, Josie and Rachel. I was glad Renee was in Mrs. Jennings' history class with us.

"Hi Renee," I said. "Know anything about a girl name Cornelia Ham?"

Renee shook her head. "Who?"

"A really tall skinny girl with messy brown hair, thick glasses and freckles," Jenny said. "So uncool."

"Does she wear brown and have pigtails?" Renee asked.

"Yes," I said. "That's the one."

"Oh," Renee said. "Gym class! She's in my gym class. I've seen her around, but never talked to her. She's always by herself, doesn't seem to have any friends."

"Well, guys," Jenny said. "Let's stop talking about this girl who doesn't exist and head into class."

Renee and I looked at each other. Sometimes Jenny just comes across as *insensitive*. I wonder how she would react if she found out that I was different as well. I wonder how any of my friends back in New York and my new friends here would react. I could not imagine telling Mom, Grandma or Peter. So far only Mrs. Potts knew that I was *gifted* with an incredible ability that even I couldn't comprehend. I only knew that I could make magical things happen, and my gift is to be used to help others.

Chapter Three

A New You

After history class, I pulled Renee aside. "When do you have gym?" I asked.

"Before lunch," Renee said. "Why?"

"Can you deliver this note to Nellie Ham?" I asked.

"Okay," Renee replied. "Can I ask what it's about?"

I hesitated. "It's just something I have to do."

"Oh, okay," Renee said.

"Well," I said. "What if I tell you I'd like to help Nellie?"

Renee laughed. "What? How?"

"By making her over. Completely. Like new."

"I'd like to see that!" Renee said. "But I think you need to be licensed as a plastic surgeon, psychiatrist, and Miss Manners first."

"Just get her to come out to my house tonight," I paused, and then winked. "Even if it means you have to bring her yourself."

"So I'm invited?"

"Yup," I said, hoping I was doing the right thing to invite Renee. "But only you and Nellie."

"I'll try," Renee said as we parted for our next class. "I can't wait to see what happens!"

"Me, too." I said chewing my lip. Somehow, I was not sure about the idea of making Nellie over.

By lunchtime I was thinking it might have been a bad idea. Renee joined me at a table for lunch.

"Well," Renee said her face looking smug, "I gave her your note."

"Thanks," I said waiting for Renee to say more about what happened. When she slowly unwrapped her sandwich and took a bite, I asked, "So did she read it? Did she say anything?"

Renee took a sip from her grape juice and worked on swallowing. Finally she said, "She read it and put it in her bag. Didn't say anything. Didn't look happy. Didn't look sad or anything." Renee opened up her bag of chips and popped some in her mouth. "I don't think she'll show, Lucy. I don't know."

"Well, we'll see tonight," I said. "At least it may be worth a try."

"Uh huh," Renee said between mouthfuls of chips.

I looked down at my own lunch. Fried rice with teriyaki chicken. I smiled. Cooking delicious meals was one way Grandma knew how to express her love for me, I know.

"Here, Renee," I said. "Have some of my Grandma's cooking."

Renee's eyes widened. "You get to have that for lunch? We have to wait until Friday nights for anything like that."

"Grandma loves to cook," I said. "She used to own a Chinese restaurant in New York. Now she cooks for us, among other things."

"How lucky," Renee said.

"I know," I said. "Sometimes I forget how lucky I am."

"So that's why you're going to try to help Nellie."

"Yup," I said. "If I can...."

"I don't know Nellie at all," Renee said, "but if I can, I'll try to help too!"

"Good," I said smiling. "Just come over for dinner."

I winked, "If you like Chinese food, we'll be having that tonight."

"I'll be there," Renee smiled, "unless my parents have plans."

"Call me if you can't make it then," I said. "Otherwise, I'll see you tonight!"

At that moment, Jenny plopped down beside me. "Samantha and I've been swapping lunch items. What do you have?" She looked at my bowl of fried rice and chicken teriyaki, an orange, and sugar cookies. "Boy, you take the cake!" Then she handed me a slice of hard frosted birthday cake that looked like it had been in the refrigerator for weeks. "And I'll have your sugar cookies."

Before I could open my mouth to protest, Jenny had left with my sugar cookies.

"I think she's finally warming up to us," Renee said.

"I think so, too," I said. "Actually, swapping desserts with her is better than swapping insults."

"I know," Renee said, referring to my first day of school, and my brush with the then hostile, but still super-spoiled Jenny.

A boy with brown hair and green eyes wearing a football jersey and jeans walked by us, and said "hi" to Renee. Renee blushed. "He's Mark Mason, a 7th grader. He lives down the street from me."

"Oh," I said. Now I know I was not the only 12 year-old girl who felt awkward around certain boys. At least I was normal in that area of my life.

By the time Mrs. Cromwell dropped me off at my house, I was so anxious about the possibility of making Nellie over and helping her fit in at school that I nearly forgot to tell Grandma about Nellie and Renee. Grandma, my mother's mother, loved hearing my stories about the kids at school.

"Good thing you tell me they will come for supper,"

she said after I was done. "Tonight, we planned to have pizza. Your mother rented for me two movies. She will pick up pizza on her way home from work. Pizza and two movies – what could be nicer? *The Sound of Music* with Julie Andrews and *Cleopatra* with Elizabeth Taylor. Can't wait to watch them tonight with popcorn and sodas."

"Pizza will be fine," I said, feeling a little disappointed.

"Okay," Grandma said. "If your friends want Chinese food, we have dumplings that I made this afternoon. I'll teach you and your friends how to boil water and cook the dumplings. Once dumplings are made, cooking the dumplings is simple," Grandma snapped her fingers loudly for emphasis. She looked so funny snapping her fingers, I laughed.

"Thank you, Grandma," I said. "I think learning to cook with you is always fun!"

Grandma laughed too. "You're just too spoiled by my fancy cooking.

I laughed. "True, you make the best Chinese food in the world!" I hugged Grandma.

Grandma chuckled. "Alright, I'll make some sweet bun pastries for you, too. Anything else?"

"Oh, do you know if we have any fabric?" I asked, remembering the purpose for tonight's special dinner.

Grandma walked over to a box in Mom's office where Mom worked on art projects for her job as an art professor at the University of California Irvine. In the corner of the room atop of a worktable was a large cardboard box with the label, "Lucy" scribbled in red ink along its side.

"A nice old lady with white hair and a crazy bright dress came by this afternoon," Grandma said. "She said she was a friend of yours. She wanted to give you some fabric for your project."

"It must be Mrs. Potts," I said.

"Yes, a Mrs. Potts," Grandma said. "Very nice. Reminds me of someone I know...but I can't remember." Grandma shook her head. "Said you were special and to take good care of you." Grandma touched my shoulder. "We already know that you are special. You're a Lee!"

"That's a relief," I said. "I thought I was a three-headed monster," I joked. So Grandma didn't know that I was a Gifted Girl yet. Thank goodness. I still didn't know what that really meant, at least not yet.

I walked up to the box. It was sealed tight. Grandma stood behind me, waiting for me to open it. I pulled out a pair of scissors and tried to cut through the tape. The scissors bounced off the tape and landed on the ground. "Strong tape," Grandma said heading for the kitchen. "I'll go find a knife. Maybe the scissors are too dull."

"That's okay, Grandma," I said carrying the box up the stairs to my room. "I think I know how to open it."

"Okay," Grandma said. "I'll start making pastries for your friends."

When I reached the top of the stairs and walked into my room, the box seemed to have doubled in size. I dropped the box on the ground and wiped my eyes. The box kept growing and growing until it was the same size as me. Finally, it stopped growing and gave a shake or two. I walked up close and touched the box, thinking it had stopped moving. As soon as I touched the box and said, "Open," all the walls of the box fell open, and a slew of fabric of all colors and texture came tumbling out. A smaller dark wood box full of ribbons, needles, and threads was lying on top of the pile. Right next to it was a red leather book - the size of a journal - with a lock shaped like my golden heart charm. "Open," I said again, thinking it was going to pop open. The book remained closed. "I think that's why there's a lock," I said to myself. "But I wonder where the key is…" I looked and looked through all the fabric, needles, ribbons, threads, and the box, but could not find a key in sight. But I did find a note written in gold ink that read:

The key to your heart is the greatest gift of all.

"I don't know what that means," I said to the box. "But I do know that I have to build a whole new wardrobe for Nellie if she's going to be made over."

I heard a knock on the door. "Telephone for you, Lucy," Grandma's voice said behind the door.

"Okay," I said. "I'll get it in Mom's room." I waited for the shuffling of feet grow fainter before I opened the door and peeked outside. How can I explain all the fabric in my room, and a box that kept growing? Then I quickly sneaked into Mom's room where she had a Victorian-inspired telephone. "Hello?" I asked.

A girl's voice softly said, " Hi, Lucy, I'm Nellie, I seemed to have gotten lost. I'm on your street, but I'm not sure which house it is."

Nellie's coming! "I'm the one facing the corner light with an American flag in front."

"Oh," Nellie said. "Oh, I see Renee walking this way. I'll just wait for her."

"Okay," I said, looking at my blue watch. "I'll see you soon, then. Good-bye." I rushed downstairs and grabbed a pair of scissors in Mom's office and raced back into my room. Then I grabbed a hot-pink silk fabric and the scissors. I closed my eyes, and prayed for quickness, and touched my golden heart necklace. In a matter of seconds, a hot-pink silk pantsuit with buttons and zippers hung in my closet. I grabbed a white and black striped soft fabric which was turned into a feminine dress. Within minutes,

I had a yellow sundress, a lavender jumpsuit, and a long tan raincoat. A white cotton sleeve dress, embroidered in Egyptian patterns along the collar and shoulders I set aside for myself.

I blinked. It worked again. I just wondered if the gift would work on someone other than me.

I gathered the rest of the fabric and tried to shove it into my closet. The fabric came tumbling out. There was just too much! Then as if sensing my need to find a place for the fabric, the walls of the box stood up and mended itself into a large box again. I shoved all the fabric in, but kept the sewing box and the leather journal out. I closed the flaps of the box and stepped aside. "Close," I said, touching my golden heart necklace. The box closed tightly and shrank down to its original size.

I laughed in delight. No wonder why Mrs. Potts enjoyed her job as a Messenger so much. It was always so fun finding a new gift.

The doorbell rang, and I rang downstairs to open it. Nellie stood outside talking with Renee. They both had smiles on their faces. Nellie had not changed from this morning at school and still wore her brown cotton dress. Renee was in jeans and a yellow sweater. In her hands, she had a bag.

"Hairspray and stuff," she said.

"Okay," I said smiling. "Come on in!"

I quickly gave Nellie the grand tour of the house and left Renee to the mercy of Grandma, who was busy finishing a new tray of pastries.

"Come," Grandma said to Renee, " I'll show you how to boil water to cook dumplings."

Renee looked at me and shrugged. "It's not everyday that you get to learn how to cook Chinese dumplings from the best Chinese cook in the world," I said. "I'll just be a minute with Nellie. I want her to try on some things."

Then I proceeded to lead Nellie to my room where the four new outfits I made for her laid on my bed.

"This is my room," I said. "I have some things I'd like to give you," I said. "I think they'll fit you."

Nellie walked into the room. "You have a nice room," she said, nervously. "It's so nice of you to invite me to your house," she said. "No one's ever invited me before."

"Well, Nellie," I said feeling more determined to help her. "There has got to be a first." I took the lavender jumpsuit over to Nellie. "Can you try this on?" I asked.

"Sure," Nellie said. "In here?"

"Sure," I said. "Or in the bathroom."

"I'll just change here," Nellie said. With that, she got out of her brown plain dress and changed into the jumpsuit that fitted her so perfectly.

I watched closely to see if there was any change in her. As she looked into the pine full-length mirror, I noticed that her back had straightened, and her shoulders were pushed confidently back. A rosy glow filled her cheeks, and her eyes brighten. "Wow," I said, "you look better already!"

"I feel better," Nellie said. "There's something about this suit that makes me feel better. I feel happier!" She took the elastic bands holding her pigtails in place out of her hair. Her long brown hair cascaded smoothly down her back as if it had been brushed a thousand times. I reached up to take her glasses off.

"Can you still see?" I asked. What a change. With the new clothes, her confidence, and no glasses, she looked like a young model in those fashion magazines.

Nellie blinked. "It'll be a miracle if I can," she said. "I've been wearing glasses for years. She blinked again. "No," she said. "I doubt I can see without them. Been wearing them since I was 7. Now I'm 14."

I sighed. Helping Nellie regain her sight is beyond my

abilities.

"I'm going to get contacts," Nellie said happily. "And a whole new wardrobe!" She turned around. "This must have cost you a fortune."

"You can have it," I said. "You can have all of these outfits. They were made for you."

"But I couldn't," Nellie said.

"They wouldn't fit anyone else I know," I said, winking. "Hey, let's show everyone how you look," I said.

Nellie looked nervous but excited. "Sure." We made our way down the stairs and into the kitchen where Renee and Grandma had cooked four plates of dumplings.

"Renee and Grandma," I said. "Dinner ready?"

"Dinner is served," Renee said laughing, busily scooping out dumplings from the pot. "Grandma taught me how to boil dumplings and even how to make the sauce. Now I can make some Chinese food, and it's fun!"

Renee and Grandma suddenly looked up and saw Nellie. "Very pretty," Grandma said nodding with a smile.

"Where's Nellie," Renee joked.

Nellie and I started laughing and gathered around the kitchen. By the time Mom and Peter came home with the pizza and movies, we were all full with dumplings and sweet pastries.

Because Nellie and Renee had to be home before eight o' clock, they left before Mom popped in the tape of *Cleopatra*. Peter fell asleep after stuffing himself with pizza so I helped Mom take him upstairs to his room. Grandma continued watching the movie, and returned to my room. My head was spinning with excitement. It worked! My ability to sew actually helped someone - to think that I had never touched a needle or a thread in my life just a few weeks ago.

I went to my dresser drawer and pulled out Muriel's map. Somehow I needed to get this back to Muriel so she could fulfill her destiny. I changed into my safari outfit, put on Muriel's jacket, and gingerly put the map into the inside pocket of my jacket. I picked up the white cotton dress that I made with the Egyptian embroidery. It was the perfect outfit for the Egyptian desert heat. Then I closed my eyes, touched my golden heart charm, and prayed to be in Egypt.

Chapter Four

Plight of The Beauty Queen

I looked around me noticing a large dark room dimly lit by burning torches on the walls. Pictures similar to the ones on Muriel's map adorned the walls in shades of brilliant gold, red, blue, and purple. I was in some chamber of some sorts. Perhaps I was in Cleopatra's tomb with Muriel and Dr. Winston?

I walked around the chamber. There were clay jars laid out all around the floor and stacks of food in the corners. I walked to the entrance of the chamber and heard voices. I looked around the corner and saw shadows of men along the wall. They were in a room next door chanting.

A young woman's voice echoed loudly against the stone walls. "I promise you I will rule Egypt as peacefully as you have ruled," she said between sobs. "And I shall make you proud, father," she said.

The chanting grew louder. Then there was silence. Then I heard some light footsteps. "There you are," a young woman's voice said in a language I somehow could understand. "I cannot stay here much longer. They will soon cover up father's tomb and seal it. We must go," the young woman said.

I turned around and saw a girl of 17 years old wearing an exquisite gold gown that showed off her slim figure. Her face was painted with thick make-up - black eye make-up and heavy red lips. Her hair was straight with bangs. On top of her head she wore a thin gold headband shaped like a snake.

I stopped. "Cleopatra?" I asked in the girl's same language.

"Yes," the girl said. "I am now Queen Cleopatra with the passing of my father and my marriage to Ptolemy. Even though we are friends, you must still address me as Queen. Although I am as humble as a servant when it comes to lessons about medicine and languages from your father. It is so good of you to visit me from Asia during my time of need. And to accompany here to such a dreadful place, a tomb. The burden of Egypt is now mine," Cleopatra sighed. "Come, Lucia, we must head back home, away from the Valley of the Kings!"

I stepped out of the shadows.

Cleopatra looked at me and laughed. "Always the jester, Lucy! That is why we are friends. You make me laugh, but you must find something more suitable to wear than this," she came up to me and touched my jacket. "This may be fine for Asia, but much too warm for Egypt." She led the way out of the tomb where a long line of dark-skinned men in loincloth and some women waited for Cleopatra.

Outside, the blinding sunlight burned our eyes. I wished I had a pair of sunglasses with me! A couple of girls in white cotton dresses splashed around in a small pool of water surrounded by palm trees at the foot of the tomb.

Cleopatra walked proudly like a queen, no signs of sadness in her step, and ascended the chariot with her chin held high. A smaller chariot carrying two young girls in white cotton dresses stopped before me. "You shall ride with us!" the girls said in unison. I hopped aboard.

"Cleopatra is now Queen," the girls said. "Ptolemy is King," one of the girls said, "but he is just a boy. 10 years-old."

"I shall like Cleopatra as Queen," the smaller of the

girls said. "She treats us well, and she see all Egyptians whether they are from Greece or Egypt as one."

"More intelligent than any of the old King's advisors, Cleopatra knows more than eight languages, including Egyptian," the tall girl said. "Even the old King did not learn Egyptian. Young Ptolemy has yet to master his own language! He is so arrogant."

"Where are we headed," I asked after the girls fell silent.

"Oh, back to Alexandria," the tall girl said. "Cleopatra's father believed in adopting the Egyptian way of burial so he fashioned a tomb for himself in the Valley of the Kings where old Egyptian Pharaohs are laid to rest." I smiled. Muriel was right about the Valley of the Kings.

"We should be about a half day's journey to Alexandria," the smaller girl said. "In time, we shall be back in the palace."

"With lots of food and entertainment to see!" they both exclaimed.

"There will be a celebration for all by the people to welcome the new King and his wife, Cleopatra. There will be much feasting and drinking," the taller girl said.

I soon forgot about my disappointment in ending up in Ancient Egypt with Cleopatra instead of in Egypt of 1954 with Muriel, Peter, and Dr. Winston. The two girls' lively chatter about the celebration in Alexandria seemed fascinating and unbelievable. As they went on and on about the celebration, their conversation then turned to beauty and science, and it seemed as if the ride back into Alexandria grew shorter and shorter. Soon we were entering the enormous stone gates of the lost city, and arriving in front of the palace where a small boy sat on a large gold throne, bored by the antics of jugglers performing before him. They juggled swords and lit torches, yet he yawned with disinterest.

When Cleopatra's chariot arrived, she walked grandly out to join the young King. He barely batted an eyelash in response to her arrival. Cleopatra surveyed the opulent display of fruits, bread, and meats laid on what seemed to be miles of red cloth embroidered in gold on tables along the courtyard. Musicians in the corner played a light merry tune. People in the courtyard, dressed in white cotton cloth and wearing heavy gold jewelry, stood awaiting a speech from their new Queen.

Finally the Queen spoke. "People of Egypt, the time of mourning have passed. We shall celebrate a new beginning for Egypt. A renewed energy and peace among all!"

With that, the people erupted with thundering agreement with cheers in support of their new Queen.

One of the girls from the chariot brought out a golden goblet encrusted with brilliant red and green stones and handed it to Cleopatra. Cleopatra lifted the goblet and announced in a strong clear voice, "To a united Egypt!"

"A united Egypt!" the crowd shouted in agreement.

"To peace!" Cleopatra announced.

"To peace!" the crowd shouted.

Cleopatra, in her gold dress and gold-dusted skin, broke out into a beautiful smile that made her appear to glow like the sun. Everyone stared at this golden vision, in awe of her beauty. When there was silence, Cleopatra took her very young husband's hand and walked over to a large food-laden table a step below their thrones before the crowd. She lifted her goblet, and drank.

"Let us no longer be sad. Let the celebration begin!"

With that, the musicians began playing livelier music, and girls wearing gold and silver beaded dresses and silver headbands danced in the middle of the courtyard.

"Come and sit with us," said the tall girl from the chariot. She took my hand and led me to a table next to

Cleopatra's. I sat down next to the girls and observed all of the laughter and merriment of the celebration. There were plenty of food and drinks. "Oh look, Penelope," the smaller girl said to the taller one, "There's your friend Rebecca sitting next to her father and brother at that far table."

"Look," Penelope said excitedly. "Kings and princesses from afar bringing gifts for Queen Cleopatra!"

I watched a procession of extravagantly dressed people bringing in golden chests, fine clothes, perfumes, and jewelry into the palace. At the very end entered a large dark-skinned man in bright orange and red clothing and a beautiful dark-skinned young woman in a purple and red gown who bowed down in front of Cleopatra.

"Greetings from Nubia!" said the man in a deep booming voice. "We bring Queen Cleopatra a fine gift!"

At that, two young dark-skinned men entered the courtyard holding a pair of golden leashes. Attached to the end of the leashes were two magnificent leopards.

"Beautiful," Cleopatra exclaimed. "A truly wonderful gift, Prince. I thank you!"

By the end of the celebration when no one could eat much further, a silence came upon the courtyard as an old man approached the Queen. He had black tangles for hair and possessed the whitest skin that turned green and blue. He stood before the Queen in the middle of the courtyard, dressed in black. In his skeletal hands he held three masks.

"Who is that terrifying man?" I asked, as my eyes opened wide.

"Corgar," Penelope said. "A conjurer. No one knows where he came from or how old he is."

Corgar bowed down before the Queen and said in a snake-like voice, "I have a special gift to show you today, my Queen." He lifted a green mask shaped like a dragon and placed it on his face. Before everyone's eyes, he transformed into a large scaly green dragon with red angry eyes. One could see fire emanating from his nostrils, and the glow of flames shooting through the gaps in its teeth.

The Queen and King Ptolemy grasped in surprised, clearly frightened of the beast.

As quickly as he had transformed into a dragon, Corgar transformed back into the old man, after removing the mask.

A silence fell upon the palace floor. Then there was laughter and applause, mainly coming from the Queen, herself.

"Let us see what other beasts you can transform yourself into," the Queen inquired.

Corgar took another mask, shaped like a handsome man, and placed it squarely upon his face. Immediately, his body grew taller and muscular, and his face transformed into a young handsome man.

"I like this one better," the Queen chuckled. The crowd started laughing along with her.

"How about this one?" Corgar asked, removing the handsome man mask and placing a red mask on. Immediately, his body shrunk, and red fur sprouted from his body. His face became contorted into a face of horror, fear, and anger. Everyone drew back in silence.

"I still liked the second one better," the Queen said.

With that, the mask flew off, and Corgar was once again the old skeletal man. Everyone clapped with approval.

"Wonderful show," the Queen said, clapping with her hands. "Wonderful show. Now if you will excuse me, I've had a long day, and I will retire. Thank you for a most magnificent celebration." The Queen stood up with the boy King and walked off followed by a procession of servants.

"That was amazing!" I said.

"A celebration party fit for a Queen," Penelope said. "How the people love Queen Cleopatra!"

Penelope and the smaller girl stood up. " We will have to go join the rest of the royal servants now." I got up and followed them out of the courtyard and into the royal rooms, where Cleopatra was having oil rubbed into her feet. When Cleopatra was laid to bed, all of the servants walked out.

"Here, you're the same size as Aeobi here," Penelope said, giving me a white cotton dress and a dark brown cloak with a hood. "We are going out to the market!"

The white cotton dress looked similar to the one I made. I returned the one Penelope gave me and changed into the one I brought from home. Then I put on the dark brown cloak. "There," Penelope said. "You look like just another Egyptian peasant girl, instead of a nobleman's daughter." The smaller girl, Aeobi, nodded in agreement. We walked along the walls and emerged outside in a street filled with artisans, soldiers, and street vendors. It was already getting dark and torches along the streets were lit with fire. The glow illuminated the path toward the marketplace.

I followed Penelope and Aeobi through the street looking at the different wares the vendors had on display. At one of the stands, I bumped into another girl wearing a dark cloak similar to mine. Her face was hidden behind the hood, revealing only the blueness of her eyes.

"I'm sorry," I said to the girl, not thinking much about it.

"Lucia?" the girl asked. "Lucy? It's me, Cleo."

I turned around and looked closer at the eyes peering out from behind the hood. It had the same dark almond-shaped eyes as the Queen's, but without the heavy black eye make-up. "It *is* you!" I said. "What are you doing out here?"

"I wanted to see how my people live," she said. "Plus, I wanted to just be a girl and have fun roaming the streets freely without my guards and servants." She smiled. "Have you tried one of these sugar candies?" She gestured for the vendor to wrap up a few and paid him. "I've never tried these, but they look delicious." She gave me a yellow one and popped a red one into her mouth. I tried mine. It tasted like gumdrops. "Delicious!" Cleo exclaimed. We walked along the street and ducked into an alley to finish the remaining gumdrops.

"When father was King, he used to have his advisers give him reports on how the people of Egypt fared. He never stepped out of his palace to observe the daily lives of his people. And his advisers always hid the truth about the true state of his kingdom. When father died, they wanted Ptolemy to rule, a 10-year-old boy, whom they can control. Needless to say, they did not want me to be Queen." Cleo shook her head. "I have many enemies and few friends." Cleo stopped. Along the walls of the alley, the dim lights from the street torches cast shadows of Cleo and me. Then I noticed another shadow – a tall figure standing ominously nearby.

I looked around me, but did not see anyone. When I turned around, Cleo was gone. The shadow of the figure disappeared from the wall as well.

I ran out of the alley and into the street. A tall dark figure walked quickly down the street hauling a smaller struggling figure. Cleo! I ran down the street after them, yelling for assistance from Penelope and Aeobi.

Luckily when the figure turned the corner, a shepherd and his flock of sheep blocked his way. That gave me time to run up to the figure, grab a long stick and whack him twice on the head. He released his grip on Cleo. Then Penelope and Aeobi ran up to the figure and pelted him with stones. Between my clubbing him on the head, and the two servant girls bombarding him with rocks, the dark figure ran off as soon as he had the chance.

"Thank you," Cleo trembled.

"Thank you, too, girls" Cleo said to Penelope and Aeobi. "I believe you have just saved my life." Then she removed her hood.

An "awe" sprouted from Penelope and Aeobi's mouth, as they and the townspeople who had gathered around the spectacle recognized Cleo as Queen Cleopatra.

Chapter Five

The Cloth of Moses and a Key

For our bravery in helping save Queen Cleopatra's life, Cleopatra held a special award ceremony in honor of Penelope, Aeobi, and myself. As we prepared for the ceremony in Penelope and Aeobi's chambers, Penelope and Aeobi's mother, Cleopatra's most favorite royal servant, prepared my hair and outfit. She washed and brushed my hair, anointing fragrant oil into every strand, then swept it up into a high ponytail. Then she laced gold and silver ribbons through my hair. She was about to take off my golden heart necklace, when I quickly stopped her.

"But we must take this off if we must put fragrant oil on your neck," she insisted.

"I just feel it needs to stay around my neck," I said awkwardly. "You see, the clasp doesn't work. It's stuck the way it is, and if I take off my necklace, I may not be able to get it back on." I cringed at how badly I lied.

"Very well," she said. "Tonight is a special night for you girls!" She smiled proudly at me and her two girls, who were busy braiding each other's hair. After we were all dressed in salmon-pink cotton dresses with silver embroidery and silver sandals, we were marched into the courtyard where many townspeople and Egyptian nobles stood.

Cleopatra sat on her throne, radiant in a long white gown with gold and red trim. Her eyes were painted with green and gold paints, and her lips were burnish red-orange. Next to her sat Ptolemy, who looked like he wanted to be anywhere else in the world except here.

Penelope, Aeobi, and I stood at the edge of the court-yard with nervous excitement. All eyes were upon us, and I suddenly felt the way I did when I had to introduce myself in class on the first day of school.

Cleopatra signaled for us to come forward. We slowly walked through the courtyard and up the steps toward Cleopatra. When we stood facing her and Ptolemy, she stood up.

"For such bravery and loyalty to Egypt," Cleopatra announced, "I will give the highest award to any servant in Egypt. For Penelope and Aeobi, I will award you your freedom. You will no longer be a servant but free women. For the fortitude of raising such brave and smart girls, I will also award the mother of Penelope and Aeobi this freedom. You may go as you please, work for anyone you please, and marry or not marry whomever you please."

With that, a Scribe handed Penelope, Aeobi, and their mother three documents.

"These are your Freedom papers," Cleopatra said with a secret smile.

I looked over at Penelope, Aeobi, and their mother. Penelope and Aeobi beamed from ear to ear. Their mother had tears in her eyes.

"And you, Lucy," Cleopatra said solemnly. "I could give you one of my leopards or a golden chariot, but I think you want something with more meaning."

I nodded.

"I believe you would like this gift. For someone who values friendship and a deep spirituality, I give you first a key."

Cleopatra handed me a small gold key containing an inscription too small for me to read. "This is the key to Inspiration. May you continuously inspire others to be Queens and Kings of their chosen destinies. My grandmother gave me this key with love, as I am now giving it to you."

She slipped the thin gold chain carrying the key over my head where it laid side-by-side with my golden heart pendant.

"That is not all," Cleopatra said. "I am giving you a cloth cut from the swaddling clothes of Moses himself." Cleopatra smiled. "Your father, a learned and spiritual man, would appreciate this," she whispered. Then she stepped back.

"Let all of Egypt see here that acts of bravery, kindness, and loyalty will be rewarded," Cleopatra said. "Even mere girls half the age of the fiercest and strongest warriors can be brave and strong. Egypt salutes these young heroines!" With that she raised her hand and pointed it to the sky.

The townspeople shouted cheers, and the nobles clapped their hands.

I blushed under all the attention. Penelope and Aeobi smiled happily at me. If only my mother, grandmother, and Peter could see this. If only my father could see this! I sighed. I will try again someday to see if I can locate him.

When the ceremony was over, I changed back into my safari clothes, put on Muriel's jacket, and walked outside the courtyard into the palace garden where rectangular plots of flowers and fig trees, pomegranates, and date palms were planted around a square pool. I sat down on one of the stone benches by a plot of date palms and stared at the dark blue and black sky. So peaceful and quiet, I thought, listening to the chirping of crickets in the darkness of the night. This adventure turned out pretty well, I thought, secretly congratulating myself. I smiled, touching my new key pendant.

Then I heard a twig snap, and felt an icy cold wind rush pass me sending chills through my bones.

"Who's there?" I asked, looking around. "I dare you

to show yourself," I said, clutching my key pendant, my reward for bravery.

A dark figure stepped out from behind a group of date palms and stepped towards me. I recognized the steely blood-shot red eyes, the long black hair, and the waxy white skin. Corgar the Conjurer stood before me with a crooked smile. "I extend my congratulations to you, my child, for receiving such a high honor."

"Thank you," I said nervously. I stepped back, keeping my eyes fastened upon the hideous figure before me.

"May I see it?" Corgar said as he leaned toward me. "The key to Inspiration? You do not know what you have there on your neck," he said slowly, inching forward. "The ancient Pharaohs had this key hidden for ages in the sands of Egypt. There are five such keys all with different gifts for the holder of the keys. I did not know that Cleopatra held this key until tonight when she gave it to you. I have been searching for it for a while...for a long while," Corgar spat a couple of steps away. "Now it is in front of me...on a little girl's neck, so simple for me to *have* it," Corgar growled. "For *me!*" He lunged toward me, snatching at my neck.

I turned my body sideways and jumped away from his outstretched hands. He was so close; I could smell his foul sulfur-like smell. He lunged again at my neck with even more determination. I tried darting out of his hand's way, but he grasped a part of Muriel's coat. He pulled me closer to him as I fought back.

Then as I reached up to touch my golden heart pendant, Corgar grasped in surprise. "The Golden Heart Gift from God," he said. "You have the Golden Heart Gift." He felled back. "You are one of God's helper, a Gifted One." His expression suddenly changed from surprise to hate. "I will not let another Gifted One escape," he said. "I will make the gift God gave you mine, and I will reverse all the Good you have committed!"

He grasped at me again, but I jumped quickly out of his way. Then he reached into his cloak and took out a mask. He placed it over his face, and was suddenly transformed. Standing before me where Corgar had stood was my father who disappeared when I was five years old. He had amazing sparkling green eyes, a strong chin, wavy light brown hair. Dressed in a tweed sports coat and a sweater underneath, he was very much the British gentleman my mother married in New York. He smiled. "Lucy," he said. "Daddy hasn't seen you in so long. How are you doing?"

I shook my head in disbelief. The resemblance was remarkable. I stared at him carefully. He had the same dimpled smile, the same perfect white teeth. He was my father, wasn't he?

"My, Lucy," he said. "You sure have grown! You were just a small little girl when I left on the expedition. Now you're practically grown up!" He laughed.

I laughed, too. Daddy was here in front of me. After seven years of not knowing where he was, he was right here in front of me.

"Now Daddy wants you to do him a big favor," he said. "Can you help Daddy out?"

I nodded my head up and down, suddenly feeling like the five-year-old girl I was when Daddy disappeared.

"Good," he said. "Can you come here to Daddy and let me see your pretty necklaces?"

I nodded my head again and began walking towards Daddy. He smiled indulgingly at me. As I got up close to him, I felt a voice within me shout, "No!" I hesitated.

Daddy's smile disappeared, and his face contorted angrily. "Lucy, I said for you to come to me!"

"No," I said.

"I *said* come to me *now*!" With that Daddy was so

angry, he tore at his face, as if he wanted his face to come off. It did come off, as a mask. Daddy shrunk back down into Corgar.

"Corgar," I said, "Not for a second did you have me believe that you were my father. He's a better man than you ever could be!" With that I touched my golden heart necklace and prayed to be home in beautiful Huntington Beach, California back with my family and friends.

Chapter Six

Home and The Maker of Masks

Once again, God answered my prayer. I stood in my room facing my window clad in my safari outfit and boots. I had Muriel's jacket on, and now I was also wearing a gold key pendant looped onto a thin gold chain around my neck. Inside Muriel's jacket pocket was the ancient map and the piece of cloth from Moses' swaddling clothes. I took off the jacket and hid it in the back of my closet. I took off my two necklaces, pulled off the pendants and combined them onto one chain that I wore around my neck. Then I changed into my pink pajamas and fell into bed. Immediately I fell into a deep sleep with nightmares of Corgar chasing me across time and far off lands.

The next morning I could barely wake up. My tossing and turning in bed kept me from sleeping well. Somehow, I managed to climb out of bed, get ready, and make it to school.

Renee and Elsie, who were managing the Liberty Quilt project in school, came by and greeted me at the entrance to the school. "Everyone is talking about Nellie Ham," Renee said. "Lucy, what did you *do* to her?"

"Suddenly, there's Nellie this, Nellie that...the school can't get enough of Nellie!" Elsie said with her short red hair bouncing in emphasis. "A couple of days ago, no one had ever heard of her! Now I've heard that a talent agent contacted her and wants her to try modeling for an agency in Beverly Hills."

"Oh, I just helped pick out some nice outfits that

brought out the best in her. Nothing much," I said nonchalantly.

"You have got to help me pick out some outfits, too!" Elsie said. "It's amazing how what you wear can change how you think about yourself or how people act towards you." She winked. "Wouldn't that be a great quote in the 6th grade section of the yearbook?"

"Wonderful," I said, thinking maybe there was some truth in that quote.

At that moment, a group of 8th grade boys walked passed us talking about how "hot" this new girl, Nellie, was.

"I can't believe how people can be so shallow!" Renee said. "Nellie went to this school for almost three years, and now people realize she's alive just because she looks like a model?"

At that moment, Nellie walked over to us. She was wearing the black and white stripe dress I made for her. Her hair was straight down, and her green eyes sparkled.

"Hi girls," Nellie beamed. "This is a beautiful day, isn't it?" Then she looked at Renee and Elsie. "Will you excuse me and Lucy, I've got to talk to her. Thanks!"

I said "bye" to Renee and Elsie, and walked over to a corner with Nellie. "Actually," Nellie said, "can we go to the girl's bathroom?"

"Sure," I said, wondering why we couldn't talk in the hallway.

We walked into the girl's bathroom, and Nellie stopped smiling. She looked around to see if there were anyone else in the bathroom. When the bathroom seemed empty enough for her, she let out a loud sigh. "Lucy, this is a nightmare!"

"What?" I asked, my eyes widening. "How? Why? I mean, what happened?"

Nellie took off her dress and reached into her backpack where she pulled out a tan dress I didn't make for her. She changed into the tan dress. Immediately, her shoulders slumped down and her facial glow disappeared. "See?" Nellie said. "I don't understand why I can't be my new self in anything other than those outfits you gave me." She shook her head. "Lucy, a modeling agency just signed me up for teen modeling. I'll have to keep changing into different clothes and everything to be a model. I won't look like a model without those special outfits you gave me! What am I going to do?"

I stepped back. I didn't think my plan on making Nellie over was going to turn out like this?

"I can't look the way I did before," Nellie wailed. "It'll be even more embarrassing now that people have noticed me. Beforehand, I didn't even exist."

I thought about it. "Nellie, I'm really sorry about all of this," I said. "I just wanted to help you feel better about yourself, not make you more embarrassed than before." I moved closer to Nellie. "Look, Nellie, what would happen if you tried standing up straighter and pulling your shoulders back like this," I said, demonstrating a straight posture like the one she had while wearing the black and white dress I made.

She stood up straighter, but remained tight and rigid. I pushed her shoulders back and used a finger to lift her chin. "There," I said smiling. "You look a lot better." Nellie didn't look as nice as she did wearing the magical outfit, but her posture improved a hundred times better than the old Nellie.

Nellie looked at herself in the mirror. "I guess," she said doubtfully.

"How about a smile?" I asked, trying to remember how Nellie was when she looked confident and happy. She cracked a small smile. I walked over and pinched her cheeks.

"Ouch!" Nellie jumped. Her cheeks turned a bright pink.

"Much better," I said. "Now when you walk and talk, just think you're beautiful," I said. "It'll make you feel beautiful if you think you are," I said.

I thought about Cleopatra, one of the most beautiful women in the world, and her confidence as a woman and as an intellectual. That day when I saw her disguised as a peasant girl on the streets, she looked just like any of the young girls in Egypt. It was the way she carried herself, the way she acted with kindness and generosity, and the way she worked at looking beautiful that made her stand out above all others.

"Think I'm beautiful," Nellie said. "Think I'm beautiful," she said. "I'm intelligent, smart, and beautiful," she said to herself in the mirror. She turned around smiling. "If I talk to myself like this everyday, I'll start to believe it."

"Yes," I said smiling. "Just practice standing straighter and taller."

"I'll try," Nellie said, suddenly looking almost as beautiful as she did when she first tried on one of my outfits.

"Good," I said. "Now when you become famous, Nellie, remember you owe it all to me, Lucy, your manager!" I joked.

Nellie started laughing, and together we walked out of the girl's bathroom, and back into the daily life at Beachside Middle School.

When the final class was over at the end of the day, I could hardly wait to go home. It felt like days since I had been at home, and I wanted to spend some time doing girls things like talking on the phone with my New York girlfriends Rachel and Josie or painting my toenails some outrageous fun funky colors. All this talk about beauty with Nellie wanted me to try something new just for fun.

When the bus pulled up at the front of the school, I went onboard. Josh and Jenny had to visit their aunt right after school so they couldn't drop me off at my house today. That was fine. I wanted to be alone with my thoughts. The bus was half-full so I picked a seat in the back. As soon as all the kids who had to take the bus were onboard, the bus drove off.

I stared outside the window at the passing trees and buildings. We passed a shopping center and a park. That was when I spotted him. Could it be?

I wasn't sure if I was here in Huntington Beach or back in Egypt. The man walking through the trees in the park, looking almost like a homeless man, had a black ragged cloak, black long hair, and waxy white skin. I could recognize him anywhere – Corgar the Conjurer. Before his red eyes could glance up at me staring horrified in the bus, the bus flew pass him.

My heart raced. The palms of my hands grew sweaty. I had to wipe them on my jeans. Life in tranquil, sunny Huntington Beach was going to change if Corgar was around. I touched my golden heart necklace and key pendant. It was up to me to stop that.

Chapter Seven
A Visit to the Gift Messenger

As soon as the bus stopped on Mulberry Lane, I got off. It has been a while since I last visited the little white house on Beachview Lane where I first discovered my Gifts. It was time that I visited the little old lady with a British accent like Mary Poppins.

When I walked up to the porch of the house, the door was opened. Mrs. Potts, wearing a yellow and orange dress, had a straw hat on her head, and a pair of gardening gloves on her hands, carried out a big pot of sunflowers.

"Hi, Lucy," she said smiling, as she placed the pot on the porch and picked up a watering can. "Sunflowers usually grow during the summers, but somehow when I planted these sunflower seeds ten days ago, they decided they wanted to grow *now* – in the fall!"

"Hi, Mrs. Potts," I said. "I haven't seen you for a while."

"I know," Mrs. Potts said. "You don't have to see me to know I'm around, though," she said with a smile. "How's my little Gifted Girl doing?"

"Well, I've been busy…"

"With your gifts, I know," Mrs. Potts said. "Come inside. Mr. Smithy's expecting you."

At that, a small bundle of black fur and excited yapping scrambled outside and landed at my feet. Mrs. Potts' friendly little black Scottish Terrier really knew how to make anyone feel welcome at Mrs. Potts' home. Mr. Smithy kept jumping up, trying to get my attention.

He stopped when I bent down and petted him behind the ears, his short tail wagging uncontrollably.

"Alright now, Mr. Smithy," Mrs. Potts said to the happy little dog, "Lucy's here to see me on some more pressing matters, isn't that so, Lucy?"

"Ummm, yes," I said.

"Then come on in and let's have a chat over some cinnamon tea and crumb cake." Mrs. Potts gave the sunflowers a light sprinkling of water from the water can and then led the way into her house.

I walked into Mrs. Potts' house. It was exactly as I had remembered it. Antique furniture, country quilts, and nice light blue walls. *Destiny's Calling*, the painting painted by a 12-year-old Emily Cobbs, a Gifted Girl from England around 1900, still hung above the fireplace. I moved closer to the painting. While the beautiful young woman with long dark hair and porcelain skin still stood against a cliff as I remembered the first time I saw the painting, something was different. I peered closely at the painting. The clouds were darker this time, and in the background, there appeared to be a door bolted shut by a large lock. The young woman in the painting now held a book in her hands and a cloth.

I jumped back. "Mrs. Potts," I called. "This is Destiny's Calling, right? You know, the one painted by Emily Cobbs."

Mrs. Potts came behind me from the kitchen where she had set a pot of water to boil. "Last I check, Lucy, it's the one and only Destiny's Calling painting by Emily Cobbs."

"It's different," I said. "Wildly different. What happened?"

Mrs. Potts started laughing. "Oh my, Lucy, have my old age gotten the best of me!" Then she wiped her eyes. "This is a 'Living Painting' that lives and adjusts to suit whoever is looking at the painting. "Isn't that a marvelous work of art," Mrs. Potts laughed. "When Emily first realized the potential of her gift, she experimented with all kinds of paintings and artwork! This is just one of those experiments. " Mrs. Potts smiled. "That is what is so amazing about the gifts of the Gifted Girls. You can do so much with it." She winked, "And besides that, it's fun."

We walked over to her antique oak kitchen table where she had placed a slice of cinnamon and sugar crumb cake on a colorful plate for me. "Try this cake," Mrs. Potts said proudly. "Another cake from Daniella's recipe book. Daniella's recipes are guaranteed to work. They're foolproof!"

I sat down and took a bite of the cake. It practically melted like sweet butter in my mouth. "This is delicious!" I said, unable to believe that this cake came from a recipe written by a 10 year-old girl living in France. "You can tell Daniella had a lot of fun with her Gifts right away!" Mrs. Potts laughed. "As a Gifted Girl, she was bold and bright." Mrs. Potts walked over and poured cinnamon honey tea into the colorful cup in front of me. Then she sat down with a cup in front of her. "So Lucy, how has it been? Are you enjoying your Gift as much as you were meant to?"

"I am enjoying it, Mrs. Potts," I started. "I mean, I've seen wonderful things, met some interesting people, lived some amazing adventures...."

"But you don't know if you're doing the right thing every time you use your Gift," Mrs. Potts finished for me.

I nodded my head in agreement. "I mean, in one adventure, I went back in time to Egypt, hoping to find my father, but I met a team of archaeologists. I did something that may have changed the outcome of their destinies," I said. "I mean, I still have the map Muriel needs to find Cleopatra's tomb."

Mrs. Potts sat in silence. "Maybe Cleopatra's tomb was never meant to be found," Mrs. Potts said thoughtfully, "and Muriel had another destiny more important than discovering Cleopatra's tomb."

"I wonder what could be more important than that?" I said.

Mrs. Potts smiled warmly at me. "There are some destinies that would definitely be more important than that one. But, there's more, isn't there?"

"Yes, there's a lot more," I said, hating how awful I felt about letting anyone know about this mishap. "I actually met Queen Cleopatra, and she awarded me the Key of Inspiration and Moses' cloth."

Mrs. Potts' eyes widened. "Then you have the Key," she said.

"Yes," I said. "I have the key, but I don't know what to do with it."

"You have a book that was sent in the 'Box that Adjusts' that I dropped off the other day?" Mrs. Potts asked. I nodded. "That key unlocks the book."

"What's in that book?" I asked.

"Wisdom," Mrs. Potts said. "Among other things...."

"Someone really wants that key pretty badly," I said, shaking my head. "I met a really evil man in one of my adventures who tried to steal my Gifts from me. His name was Corgar the Conjurer."

Mrs. Potts' eyes looked a little alarmed. "The Maker of Masks," she said. "He makes masks of deception, trying to bring out the worst in people." She took a sip from her cup. "I can see why he wanted your Gifts. You're doing good work and succeeding in it! While he's trying to make people feel angry, sad, or fearful; you're being used by God to help people around you feel better about themselves, lift themselves up." Mrs. Potts smiled. "The fact that Corgar feels threatened by you means that you're doing exactly what you're supposed to be doing."

"The only problem is," I said, feeling relieved, "he's here in our town. Somehow, he has found his way into my time period and my hometown. And I want him *out!*"

Mrs. Potts looked alarmed now. "That is not good."

"What can I do?" I asked. "I can't keep using my golden heart necklace to run away from him."

"I don't know," Mrs. Potts said, looking down. "I'm a Gift Messenger. I help deliver gifts from God. I don't know how to fight a Mask Maker."

"I fought him once when he pretended to be my father," I said. "Somehow, I had the strength to see through Corgar's tricks. I don't know how I did that, though."

Mrs. Potts stood up, gathering the empty plates. "Emily Cobbs once fought Corgar when he entered her time period and town. She sent him back to the Middle Ages where they nearly burned him at the stake. I think it's time you met Emily Cobbs," Mrs. Potts said smiling. "Knowing Emily, she wouldn't mind sharing a thing or two about being a Gifted Girl."

I got up, my confidence now renewed. "I think that's what I'll do," I said, grabbing my backpack. I kissed Mrs. Potts on the cheek. "Thanks for believing in me," I said. "I've got to go now. Thanks again!"

With that, I headed out the door and into the quiet, peaceful street. The sky outside had turned gray with dark charcoal clouds. It looked like there was going to be rain. Remembering my way home, I quickened my pace. By the time I reached the curb of my home, the sky had turned black. Little drops of water fell on my head. I rushed quickly onto my porch before a cloud burst of heavy raindrops came pouring down.

When I opened the front door of my house and stepped inside, Mom, Grandma, and Peter were sitting in the kitchen.

"Hi everyone," I said, putting my backpack on the ground. "It is pouring outside! Have you seen this, Peter?"

Peter rushed over to the living room window and peered outside. "Wow, this is cool!"

"Not if you're caught in the downpour," I said. "Which I nearly was."

"Then you don't have to take a shower!" Peter said laughing like a hyena. "Not that you ever do," he said.

I rolled my eyes at him. Then I reached over, rumpled his already messy hair, and gave him a hug, which surprised him completely. Nothing like an obnoxious little brother to remind me I'm still just a girl.

"Lucy," Mom said from the kitchen. "Will you come here for a second?"

"Sure, Mom," I said, releasing Peter, who hurried back over to the window, wanting to see more of the downpour. I walked over to where Mom and Grandma sat reading mail in the kitchen.

Mom looked at me, her eyes tired. "Lucy, this came for you," she said, handing me a light thin pink envelope.

I looked at the address. Mrs. Frankford P. Lee from London, England. The envelope was addressed to: Miss Lucy Tiffany Lee. "This is from Daddy's mother, isn't it?" I asked.

"Yes," Mom said. "Your Grandmother in England, who was too ill to see you when you were born, and suffered a stroke when she heard about your father. She never made it out to see us in America after that." Mom looked down at the envelope I held in my hands. "Why don't you open it?"

"Okay," I said, feeling self-conscious. A letter from the Grandmother I have never met. I gingerly open the delicate envelope, and pulled out a thin letter and read it silently.

Dear Lucy Tiffany,

I believe now you are 12 years old. It's been far too long that I have not seen my only son's little girl. Unfortunately, due to my condition since you were born, I have not been well enough to travel across to America. But I would dearly love to see you and your little brother.

I will soon wire your mother some money to buy plane tickets for you and your brother to spend Christmas with me in London. I believe you have some time off from your studies then. Until then, I hope all is well with your mother.

Love,
Your Grandmother
Florence "Muriel" W. Lee

"Mom!" I screamed. "Peter and I are going to London!" I thrust Grandmother's letter under her nose. "To visit Grandmother," I said, dancing.

Peter rushed into the kitchen near me. "What? We're going to England? Where Father came from?"

"Yup," I said, breaking out into a little dance. "Grandmother Lee's paying for our tickets to go visit her for Christmas!" Grandmother Florence "Muriel" W. Lee. Muriel? I stopped dancing, and turned to Mom. "Mom, do you know anything about Grandmother Lee?"

Mom turned towards me, placing the letter down. "Well, honey, since you and Peter are going to visit her soon, you might learn more about her." Mom stood up. "Your Grandmother Lee was the smartest young woman in London in the 1950s. Had lots of potential. Could've done anything she wanted – politics, law, whatever. She went into archaeology for a while at a very young age with her Father, Dr. Terence Winston, but soon fell in love with an American - your Grandfather - who struck it rich selling antique artwork in Europe. When your Grandfather passed away at a young age, Grandmother Lee took over the art business and became very protective of your father." Mom sighed. "She hasn't exactly warmed up to me, but she'll love to see you and Peter. She's a brilliant woman." Mom stopped and got out some mugs. "Nothing like sipping warm hot chocolate with marshmallows on a rainy day." She smiled. "Does that answer your question about your grandmother?"

More than enough, I wanted to say. "Yes, it sure did," I said. Muriel Winston was my Grandmother! That was what Mrs. Potts meant when she said that Muriel's destiny was not to discover Cleopatra's tomb, but something far more important. Muriel Winston's destiny was to become my father's mother. More importantly to me, she was to become my grandmother. I smiled. I was getting closer to learning more about my father, and getting closer to learning more about the potential of my Gifts.

Excerpt from Book 1 of the Emily Cobbs Gifted Girls® Series:

Emily Cobbs
and The Naked Painting

"Emily Cobbs!" a shrilled voice called out from the parlor downstairs. No doubt it was Aunt Nell, calling me to run one of her many errands or do one of her several chores. I never know which since they often blend in together.

I looked at myself in the pine oval full-length mirror. My long curly blond hair was brushed. So full was it that it tumbled all over my face. The color was as bright as corn. How fitting, I thought to myself, that my surname was Cobbs, as in corn-on-the cob. No wonder my friend Tommy teased me to no end, often referring to my hair as a "lion's mane". I grabbed a blue satin ribbon from my dresser top and tied my hair back. There - my hair was almost neatly tucked behind my ears. My blue dress with white lace was neat and straight. My blue eyes were bright and clear. At least I looked presentable enough for whatever it was Aunt Nell wanted me to do just now.

I opened my bedroom door a crack, and said loudly enough for Aunt Nell to hear, "Coming." Aunt Nell, who really wasn't an aunt, but my father's aunt, was getting on in age. She was still strong, but sometimes her hearing was not as clear. Nonetheless, Aunt Nell was active in her many social causes, having been the wife of a Fellow at Cambridge University.

Although Uncle William had been gone a while, Aunt Nell lived in a nice English cottage within the

University grounds. It was a comfortable cottage with a vegetable garden in the back and a flower garden in front. Inside, it was roomy enough for a Fellow to entertain several guests at the dinner hall or have a cozy one-on-one chat with a colleague in the parlor.

Since it was just Aunt Nell and I in the house, with a visit twice a week from Doris, who cleans our house, the house seemed rather large.

"Emily Cobbs, this is the second time I have to call you. Where are you, child?" the scratchy voice shrilled again.

"Coming, Aunt Nell," I called again. With that, I opened my door widely and bounded down the stairs much too quickly, so quickly that my feet which seem to have grown, nearly ran on top of each other.

Suddenly, Aunt Nell's orange and white cat, Persnickel, darted in front of my feet like a mad cat obsessing over a rogue mouse. Whatever Persnickel's intentions of darting out in front of me was, as I made my awkward descent down the ridiculously curved staircase, soon flew out my mind, as I found myself falling heads first down to the bottom of the stairs.

Join the Gifted Girls® Club!

Sign up at: http://www.giftedgirls.net
Find out interesting trivia about each Gifted Girl, learn about the people, places and times in history a Gifted Girl visits. Be the first to receive the latest Gifted Girls® books, jewelry, gifts, dolls, and fun fashion accessories!

Tell your friends about Gifted Girls® and start a Gifted Girls® Group where you can read books, perform fun activities, and more!

The Gifted Girls Series®

Don't miss any of the Gifted Girls' Adventures!
Ask your bookseller for a copy today or...
Order or Reserve Your Very Own Copy Today by Mail
or online at http://www.sparklesoup.com

___ **Lucy and the Liberty Quilt: Book 1 $7.95**
___ **Lucy and the Beauty Queen: Book 2 $6.95**
___ **Emily Cobbs & The Naked Painting: Book 1 $6.95**

Meet Emily Cobbs, a Gifted Girl from turn-of-the-century (20th Century) England, who has a gift with the brush.
___ **Emily Cobbs & The Secret School: Book 1 $6.95**
___ **Gifted Girls® Activities Guide for**
    365 Days of the Year $19.95

Sparklesoup Studios
P.O. Box 2285, Frisco, TX 75034

Please send me the books I have checked above. I am enclosing
$_____ (please add $3.50 to cover shipping and handling). Send check or money order - no cash or C.O.D.'s please.

Name_____

Address_____

City_____State/Zip_____

Email Address_____
Please allow four to six weeks for delivery.

The Gifted Girls Series®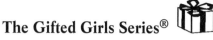

Don't miss any of the Gifted Girls' Adventures!
Ask your bookseller for a copy today or...
Order or Reserve Your Very Own Copy Today by Mail
or online at http://www.sparklesoup.com

___ **Lucy and the Liberty Quilt: Book 1 $7.95**
___ **Lucy and the Beauty Queen: Book 2 $6.95**
___ **Emily Cobbs & The Naked Painting: Book 1 $6.95**

Meet Emily Cobbs, a Gifted Girl from turn-of-the-century (20th Century) England, who has a gift with the brush.
___ **Emily Cobbs & The Secret School: Book 1 $6.95**
___ **Gifted Girls® Activities Guide for**
   365 Days of the Year $19.95

Sparklesoup Studios
P.O. Box 2285, Frisco, TX 75034

Please send me the books I have checked above. I am enclosing
$_____ (please add $3.50 to cover shipping and handling). Send check or money order - no cash or C.O.D.'s please.

Name_____

Address_____

City_____State/Zip_____

Email Address_____
Please allow four to six weeks for delivery.